Presented to

_____

With love from

_____

Date

_____

Welcome to *The Story* — God's Story

This book tells the grandest, most compelling story of all time: the story of a true God who loves his children, who established for them a way of salvation and provided a route to eternity. Each of these 31 stories reveals the God of grace — the God who speaks; the God who acts; the God who listens; the God whose love for his people culminated in his sacrifice of Jesus, his only Son, to atone for the sins of humanity.

What's more: this same God is alive and active today — still listening, still acting, still pouring out his grace on us. His grace extends to our daily foibles; our ups, downs, and in-betweens; our moments of questions and fears; and most importantly, our response to his call on our lives. He's the same God who forgave David's failures and rescued Daniel from the lions' den. This same heavenly Father who shepherded the Israelites through the wilderness desires to shepherd us through our wanderings, to help us get past our failures and rescue us for eternity.

It's our prayer that these stories will encourage you to listen for God's call on your life, as he helps write your own story.

— Max Lucado and Randy Frazee

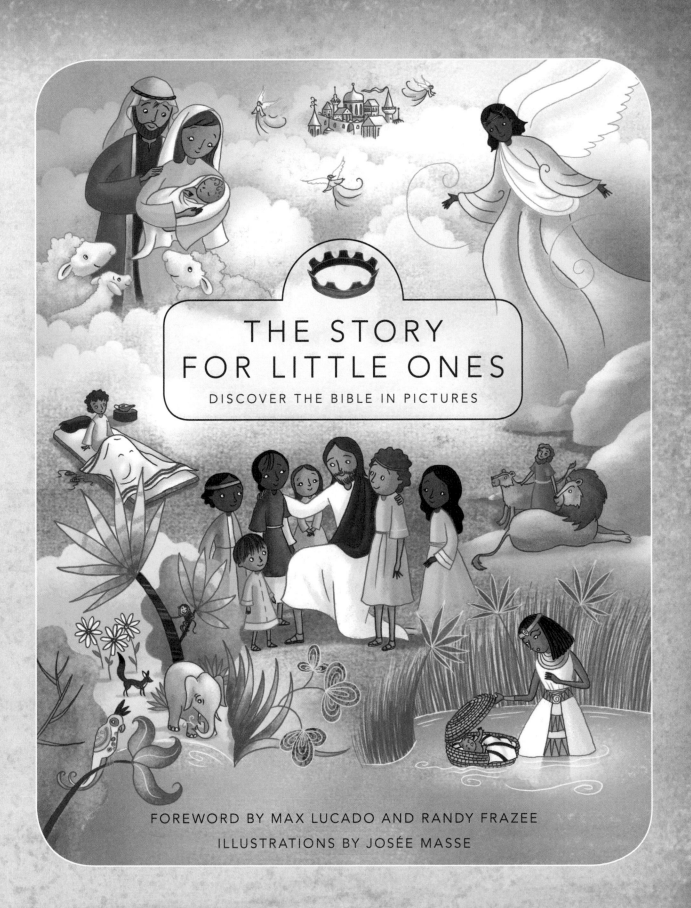

THE STORY FOR LITTLE ONES

DISCOVER THE BIBLE IN PICTURES

FOREWORD BY MAX LUCADO AND RANDY FRAZEE

ILLUSTRATIONS BY JOSÉE MASSE

ZONDER**kidz**

ZONDERVAN.com/
AUTHORTRACKER
follow your favorite authors

To my dear mother with all my love.
–J.M.

ZONDERKIDZ

The Story for Little Ones
Copyright © 2011 by Zonderkidz
Illustrations © 2011 by Josée Masse

Requests for information should be addressed to:

Zondervan, 3900 *Sparks Drive, Grand Rapids, Michigan* 49546

Library of Congress Cataloging-in-Publication Data

The Story for little ones : discover the Bible in pictures / illustrated by Josée Masse.
        p.   cm.
    ISBN 978-0-310-71927-4 (hardcover)
    1. Bible stories, English. I. Masse, Josée.
    BS551.3.S775 2011
    220.9'505—dc22   2011005371

Contributors: Jill Gorey and Marianne Haring
Editor: Barbara Herndon
Art direction and design: Kris Nelson

Printed in China

14 15 16 17 18 19 /LPC/ 25 24 23 22 21 20 19 18 17 16 15 14 13 12 11

Table of Contents

CHAPTER 1

In the Beginning

Genesis 1–2

A long, long time ago, there was nothing. Then God spoke: "Let there be light." And there was light! God called the light day, and he called the darkness night. God said the light was good.

Next, God made the sky, the land, and the oceans. God smiled when he saw that everything he made was good.

Then God said, "Let there be plants. And trees with fruit and seeds.
Let the sun, moon, and stars shine in the sky, and let birds and animals appear."
And everything happened just like God said, and it was all good.

Then God did something different. He picked up the dust on the ground and made a man. He breathed air into his lungs. He called the man Adam. Then God made a woman. He named her Eve. God made people to be his children. He blessed them and said that what he made was very good.

God was happy with everything he made. Then God rested because his work was done.

God made Adam and Eve.
God made you too.
Isn't it wonderful to be a child of God?

Abraham Follows God

Genesis 12:1–9; 15:1–6; 21:1–7

Abraham was a good man who trusted God. God told Abraham, "I want you to leave your home and your country and go to a new land I will show you."

Going to a new place was scary, but Abraham chose to trust God.

Abraham and his wife, Sarah, packed up all their things. They gathered their sheep and cattle and traveled a long way. They took everyone in their house, including Abraham's nephew Lot and all of his animals.

When they arrived in the new land, Abraham and Lot could not find enough food for all their animals.

Again, Abraham chose to trust God. "Lot," Abraham said, "you can have the best land, and I will move to a different place." And he did.

God told Abraham that Abraham and Sarah would have a baby. That was hard to believe because Abraham and Sarah were old!

Abraham chose to trust God. When Abraham was 100 years old, Sarah had a baby boy, and they named him Isaac.

Abraham trusted God.
You can trust God too. He is always by your side.

Joseph Forgives His Brothers

Genesis 37; 39–45

Isaac had a son named Jacob. When Jacob grew up he had many sons, but his favorite was Joseph. Jacob gave Joseph a colorful robe. This made Joseph's brothers mad.

One night, Joseph had a dream. Stars and grain bowed down to him, like he was a king! Joseph told his brothers about his dream. "Some day you will bow down to me too!" This made Joseph's brothers even madder. They stole Joseph's robe, put him in a deep hole, and sold him! Joseph became a slave in Egypt, but God had a plan for Joseph.

Pharaoh ruled all of Egypt. One day Pharaoh had a dream. Joseph told Pharaoh, "Your dream means there will be lots of food for seven years, but no food for seven years after that." Pharaoh believed Joseph and put him in charge of the whole land of Egypt. Joseph made sure there was enough food for everyone.

Joseph's brothers heard there was food in Egypt, so they went there. When they saw Joseph, they told him, "We're very sorry for what we did to you, Joseph." Joseph forgave them because he knew what had happened was part of God's plan.

God took care of Joseph.
God will take care of you too!

CHAPTER 4

God Protects Moses

Exodus 1–12

Years passed, and there was a new pharaoh in Egypt. By now, there were many, many people in Jacob's family. Pharaoh was afraid of them. He made them work like slaves. He did not let them keep their baby boys.

One mother hid her baby boy from Pharaoh. "God," she prayed, "please take care of my baby." She put him in a basket and set the basket in the river. The baby's sister watched from the reeds to make sure her brother was safe.

Pharaoh's daughter saw the basket floating down the river. She rescued the baby, named him Moses, and raised him as her own son.

God watched over Moses and his special people, the Israelites, in Egypt.
When Moses grew up, God appeared to him in a burning bush. God told Moses,
"Lead my people away from Pharaoh."

Moses did what God said. He went to Pharaoh and said, "Let God's people go."

Pharaoh said, "NO!"

Then God made many bad things happen in Egypt. Frogs filled the houses. Bugs ate the plants. The animals got sick, and the people died. Pharaoh saw that God was in charge. He finally let God's people leave Egypt.

God watched over his people.
God watches over you too.

CHAPTER 5

The Ten Commandments

Exodus 20

Moses led God's people through the desert to a mountain. Thunder rumbled and lightning lit up the sky. A thick cloud covered the mountain. A loud trumpet blasted and the mountain shook! Through the clouds, Moses heard God's voice: "Come up to me on the mountain." Moses obeyed.

On the mountain, God gave Moses rules for the people to follow.

Give God first place in your life.

Do not worship anyone or
anything but God.

God's name is special.
Use God's name with respect.

Save one day each week to rest
and spend time with God.

Respect and obey your
father and mother.

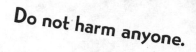

Do not harm anyone.

Mothers and fathers should keep their promises to each other.
Act with love and keep your promises.

Do not steal. Treat other people's things with respect.

Tell the truth.

Be happy with who you are and what you have.

God gave these rules to help his people live good lives and be closer to him. God's rules will help you too.

CHAPTER 6
Two Believing Men

Numbers 13

While the Israelites roamed in the desert, God told Moses, "Send men to spy on the land I promised you."

So Moses sent twelve spies into the land to see what it was like and what kind of people lived there. He made Caleb and Joshua the leaders. "Be brave," Moses told the spies. "And bring back some fruit to show us what grows in the land."

The spies went into the land and looked around for many days.

When they returned, they told God's people, "The land is beautiful! It has plenty of food."

"Hurray!" shouted God's people.

Caleb said, "Let's go live in the land now!"

But the other spies were worried. "Wait! We saw giants there! They are strong and will hurt us!"

God's people were scared. They did not want to go into the land God had promised them.

"God is stronger than any giant. He will give the land to us," Joshua said.

"God will lead us. Don't be afraid," Caleb added.

But God's people would not listen. They would not go into the land God had promised them. Because Caleb and Joshua believed in God's promise, when they were older they did go into the Promised Land.

Caleb and Joshua believed God's promise.
God keeps his promises to you.

CHAPTER 7

God's Helper

Joshua 1–6

God chose Joshua to lead his people into the Promised Land. One of the towns in that land was Jericho. Jericho had a high wall around it. Joshua sent spies to see if the city was safe to enter.

When the king of Jericho heard about the spies, he told his soldiers, "Go, capture them!"

God helped the spies by sending them to a woman named Rahab. She hid the spies in her house.

When the soldiers came, she told them, "The spies are gone, but you can catch them if you hurry!" So the soldiers hurried away.

Rahab quickly hung a rope outside of her window. She told the spies, "Now you can climb down and escape!" The spies thanked Rahab and promised to remember her.

When God's people were ready to capture Jericho, they marched around the city walls for seven days. Then the priests blew their trumpets loudly, the people shouted, and Jericho's walls fell down! The land God had promised his people was now theirs!

The spies remembered their promise and helped Rahab and her whole family.

God had Rahab help his people.
You can be a helper too.

CHAPTER 8

A Strong Man

Judges 16

There was a man named Samson who led Israel. He was stronger than all the other men. He even fought a lion and won! Samson listened to what God said, and God always helped Samson.

One day Samson fell in love with a pretty woman named Delilah. He stopped listening to God and started listening to Delilah instead.

Some bad men wanted to know what made Samson strong. They told Delilah they would give her money if she could find out his secret.

Delilah asked Samson, "What makes you so strong?"

Samson told her, "If you cut my hair, I won't be strong anymore."

When Samson was sleeping, Delilah cut his hair. Samson became weak.
The bad men came and captured Samson and put him in jail. Samson was in jail
for so long his hair started to grow back again.

The bad men were so happy that Samson wasn't strong anymore, they had a party in the temple. They brought Samson so they could tease him and make fun of him.

Samson asked God, "Please make me strong one more time." God helped Samson. God made Samson so strong he was able to knock down the thick pillars that held the building up, and the temple fell down!

Samson asked God to help him.
You can ask God for help too.

CHAPTER 9
Two Kind People

Ruth 1–4

In the town of Bethlehem in the land of Israel, there was no rain for a long time. Without the rain, nothing could grow, and there was no food. Naomi and her husband and two sons moved to a different country. After many years, Naomi's husband and sons died.

Naomi told her sons' wives, Ruth and Orpah, "I am going back to Bethlehem. You can stay here with your families. They will take care of you." But Ruth loved Naomi and said, "No, I won't leave you! Wherever you go, I go!"

So Ruth and Naomi went back to Bethlehem. They had no food, no money, and no family left to care for them. Ruth went to a field and picked up little leftover pieces of grain to feed Naomi and herself.

A kind man named Boaz owned the field. When he saw how hard Ruth worked in his field to feed Naomi, he told his workers, "Give her all the grain she wants!"

Ruth and Boaz fell in love and got married. They had a baby boy. Naomi was the baby's grandma. God blessed them with a brand-new family!

Ruth was kind to Naomi,
and Boaz was kind to Ruth.
God smiles when you are kind!

CHAPTER 10

God Hears Hannah and Samuel

1 Samuel 1, 3

Hannah wanted a baby. She went to the temple and prayed to God. "Please let me have a baby. I promise he will grow up to be your special worker."

God heard Hannah's prayer. Before long, Hannah had a baby boy and named him Samuel.

Hannah taught Samuel about God. When Samuel was older, Hannah took him to the temple where he could work for God. An important man at the temple named Eli took care of Samuel.

One night, Samuel heard a voice call his name. Samuel got out of bed and went to Eli.

"Here I am, Eli!" Samuel said.

"I didn't call you," Eli said. "Go back to bed." So Samuel went back to bed.

This happened three times. Then Eli told Samuel, "Now I understand. God is talking to you. The next time he calls your name, say, 'Speak, Lord. I am listening.'"

Samuel went back to bed. When he heard his name again, he did what Eli told him.

God heard Hannah and Samuel.
God hears your prayers too.

CHAPTER 11
David and the Giant

1 Samuel 17

One day a boy named David went to visit his brothers who were in King Saul's army.

When David reached the army camp, a giant named Goliath appeared in front of the soldiers. "Who will fight me?" the giant roared.

The soldiers shook with fear. Nobody could beat that giant!

But David wasn't afraid. "God is on our side! I'll fight the giant!"

When King Saul heard this, he told David, "You are a brave boy, but you are too young."

"I am brave because of God's help. God helps me keep my sheep safe from wild animals," David said. "He saved me from a lion and a bear! He will save me from a giant too!"

The king gave David a helmet and special clothes to protect him. But the special clothes were too heavy, so David took them off. He pulled out his slingshot and found five smooth stones along the stream.

"I come in the name of the Lord," David shouted at the angry giant.
David put a stone in his sling and flung it with all his might. The stone hit the giant right on his forehead! The giant fell to the ground with a crash. David beat the giant!

God helped David be brave.
You can ask God to help you be brave too.

CHAPTER 12

David Is Sorry

1 Samuel 18, 20; 2 Samuel 5, 9

Many years later, David became the king of God's great nation! As a king, David won many battles. With God's help, he defeated all the bad people in the area. Then the people in the kingdom lived in peace.

King David was kind and brave and loved God with his whole heart. He took care of a boy named Mephibosheth who could not walk. David wrote many songs and poems to praise God. He made plans to build God a beautiful temple.

King David did good things when he listened to God. But one day, David didn't listen to God and made a big mistake. He fell in love with another man's wife. A messenger named Nathan showed David his mistake, and David was sorry. He wrote a song to God, asking God to forgive him, and God did.

God will forgive your mistakes,
if you tell him you are sorry.

CHAPTER 13
Wise King Solomon

1 Kings 3, 9–10

King David had a son named Solomon. Solomon became the next king of Israel.

One night God appeared to King Solomon in a dream. God said, "Ask me for anything you want, and I will give it to you!"

King Solomon said, "I want to know what is right and what is wrong." God made King Solomon very wise, and he gave Solomon riches and honor too.

King Solomon had a lot of ideas about how to live a good life. He knew about all kinds of things, like plants and animals. King Solomon wrote down all the wise things he thought about.

People came from all over the world to ask King Solomon questions. One day, a queen from a faraway kingdom came to see him. She asked Solomon the hardest questions she could think of, and Solomon answered them all. "You are so wise!" the queen said. "We will praise the Lord your God for all he has done for you."

Solomon asked God to help him
know right from wrong.
God will help you make the right choices too.

CHAPTER 14

The Split in the Kingdom

1 Kings 14–15

For many years, Solomon was a wise and good king. Then he made a big mistake. He stopped listening to God. Instead of worshipping God, Solomon began to worship idols made of wood and stone.

When King Solomon died, his son Rehoboam became king. Rehoboam did not listen to God either. He made the people work hard and pay a lot of money to live in his land. The people became tired and angry. Finally, some of them

decided to leave and start a new country. God's wonderful kingdom was split in two! One country was called Israel; the other was Judah.

There was a lot of fighting between Israel and Judah. Over the years, both countries had good kings who worshipped God and bad kings who worshipped idols.

Many years later, Rehoboam's grandson Asa became the king of Judah. Asa was a good king. He loved and worshipped God and got rid of all the idols.

King Asa learned from his grandfather's mistakes.
You can learn from mistakes and do what is right.

CHAPTER 15

Elijah and Elisha

1 Kings 17–18; 2 Kings 2, 5

A bad king named Ahab became king of Israel. Ahab did not believe in God, so God sent a man named Elijah to talk to Ahab. Elijah loved God very much. Elijah's job was to tell people what God said.

God wanted to let King Ahab know that gods made of wood or stone had no power. God told Elijah, "Tell Ahab that I will not let it rain for a long, long time." When Elijah told Ahab what God said, it made Ahab very mad!

Then God told Elijah, "Run far away from Ahab so you will be safe!" God helped Elijah. He sent birds with bread and meat for Elijah to eat. Elijah drank water from a brook. No rain fell for three years.

Finally, God told Elijah to go back to Ahab and tell him that God would send rain now. The rain came. God showed Ahab that God is God, and only he has the power to make it rain!

When Elijah got old, a farmer named Elisha became his helper. One day God helped Elijah and Elisha cross a river. Elijah rolled up his coat and hit the water with it. The water divided into two parts with a dry path in the middle! Elijah and Elisha walked across on dry ground.

Then God sent a horse and a chariot for Elijah. The horse and chariot glowed brightly. Elijah rode on the chariot to heaven!

God helped Elijah and Elisha.
God will help you too.

CHAPTER 16
Messages from God

Isaiah 33, 6–7, 40

One day a man named Isaiah had a dream about God. God sat on a throne, like a king. He wore a long robe that filled the whole room. Next to God were angels with wings. As the angels sang, "Holy, holy, holy!" smoke filled the room, and the house shook. An angel came over to Isaiah and touched his lips. Then God spoke, "Who will talk to my people for me?"

Isaiah quickly shouted, "I'll go! Send me!"

Isaiah knew God's people were not obeying God. God wanted Isaiah to tell the people to stop doing bad things and to do what is right.

Isaiah told the people but they would not listen. He talked to them for many years. Still, they would not listen.

God punished his people but did not give up on them. God let Isaiah see what was going to happen in the future. God told Isaiah that someone special would be born who would teach his people how to live. He was talking about Jesus being born in the future. Everything happened like Isaiah said it would.

God doesn't give up on his people.
God won't give up on you.

CHAPTER 17

God's Prophets

Jeremiah 1:4–10, 18:1–6, 29:1–23

Years passed and still God's people were doing things that were wrong.
One day God told Jeremiah, "I have chosen you to talk to my people for me."
Jeremiah couldn't believe it. "Me?! But I'm too young!"
"Don't worry," God replied. "I will tell you what to say."

God told Jeremiah to go to a potter's house. The potter was making a pot out of clay, but it did not look good. The potter used the same ball of clay and started over again. God told Jeremiah, "My people are like that clay pot. They are not good now, but I will help them be better."

Jeremiah talked to God's people for many, many years. But God's people wouldn't listen. Jeremiah told the people that God would punish them if they continued to do wrong. But Jeremiah also said that God still loved his people and would not give up on them. God had a great plan for their future.

God loved his people even when they did wrong.
God always loves you.

CHAPTER 18

Ask God for Help

Daniel 6

God sent his people to be ruled by a different nation. A man named Darius became the new king. Daniel was the best helper in King Darius' kingdom. Because the king liked Daniel best, some of the other helpers wanted to harm him. They decided to trick King Darius into getting rid of Daniel. The angry helpers knew that Daniel prayed to God every day, so they came up with a plan.

"King Darius," they said, "you are such a great and wonderful king. You should make a new law. The law will say, for thirty days, nobody can pray to anyone but King Darius." This sounded good to the king, so he agreed.

Daniel heard the law, but he loved and trusted God. Nothing could stop him from praying to God. Not even King Darius!

The king's helpers spied on Daniel and caught him praying. Daniel was thrown into a den with lions.

Poor Daniel. The lions growled and stared at him hungrily.

Daniel was not afraid. He trusted God to take care of him.

The next morning, King Darius went to the lions' den. He removed the rock and called, "Daniel, did your God save you from the lions?"

"Yes!" replied Daniel. "God sent an angel to shut the mouths of the lions! God saved me."

King Darius was very happy. He told his servants to lift Daniel out of the lions' den. Then he told everyone in the kingdom to worship Daniel's God.

Daniel trusted in God, and God helped him.
You can trust in God too.

CHAPTER 19

God's House

Ezra 3:7–6:22

King Cyrus was a good king. God told King Cyrus to let the people go back home to Jerusalem. It was time for God's people to build a temple. God's people were very happy.

"Hurray!" they shouted.

God's people started to build the temple. They worked very hard. But after they finished the foundation of the temple, God's people stopped working on it. Instead, they started working on their own houses and planting food for their own families.

"You must work on my temple first," God told them. "Don't worry about yourselves. I will make sure you all have food and a place to live."

When the temple was finished, the people said, "This temple belongs to God! And we belong to God! We will obey and worship him. We are his people."

God's people promised to follow God.
God wants you to follow him too.

Esther Gets Ready

Esther 2–8

Esther was a beautiful woman who lived in Persia. She was one of God's people—the people of Israel. They were called Jews. The king chose Esther to be his new queen.

But the king didn't know that Esther was Jewish!

During this time, the king chose a man named Haman to work for him. Haman disliked the Jews. He found a way to make a law that would get rid of them. God's people were in danger!

When Esther found out about the law, she knew she had to talk to the king to save God's people. Queen Esther was afraid. She prayed to God, "Please help me be brave for your people." God helped Esther come up with a plan.

Esther invited the king to a big dinner. She told him to bring Haman too.
At the dinner, Esther turned to the king and said, "Please don't hurt me or my
people!"

"Who wants to hurt you?" the king asked. Esther pointed to Haman.

"Haman wants to get rid of the Jews," Esther said. "I am Jewish."

The king was angry with Haman and punished him. Then the king wrote a
new law to keep God's people safe.

God helped Esther with a hard job.
God will help you too.

CHAPTER 21

Set Apart to Honor God

Nehemiah 2–4

Nehemiah worked for the king of Persia. He tasted the king's wine to make sure it was safe for the king to drink. Nehemiah kept the king safe from harm. And God kept Nehemiah safe.

One day, Nehemiah found out that the wall around the city of Jerusalem was broken down. In those days, if a city didn't have a wall around it, the people

were in danger. Bad people could enter the city and attack them. Nehemiah was sad, because God's people were not safe, and he had grown up in that special city.

Nehemiah prayed to God. Then Nehemiah asked the king if he could go home to help rebuild the wall.

The king said, "Yes, Nehemiah. You may go!" So Nehemiah returned to Jerusalem.

Nehemiah asked God to help him find a way to keep the workers safe while they rebuilt the wall. He told the workers, "God is on our side. He will help us."

Nehemiah divided the workers into two groups. Half of the men worked on the wall, the rest kept watch to make sure no one tried to hurt them. Soon, the wall was done!

Nehemiah knew God was on his side.
God is on your side too.

CHAPTER 22
Baby Jesus

Luke 1–2; Matthew 1:18–25, 2:1–12

One day, an angel came to a girl named Mary. The angel said, "God has chosen you to have a special baby. He will be God's Son. He will save all people from their sins. His name will be Jesus."

"I will do what God wants!" Mary said.

Many months later, Mary and her husband, Joseph, traveled to a town called Bethlehem. The town was crowded with people, and all of the inns were full. There was no place to spend the night, except a stable where animals were kept. It didn't have a bed, so Mary lay down on the hay near the cows and sheep. That night, Jesus was born!

Nearby, shepherds were watching their flocks in the fields. Suddenly, angels appeared, lighting up the night sky. "The Son of God is born! Go see him!" the angels shouted with joy. The shepherds went to see baby Jesus.

Everyone was so happy. The Son of God was born!

God sent his Son to save all people.
You can trust Jesus to help you too.

CHAPTER 23

The Power of God

Matthew 3:13–17; Mark 1:9–11

Jesus had a cousin named John who baptized people. Many people came to John to talk about God and to be baptized in the river. John dipped them in the water to show that God had the power to wash away anything they had done wrong.

Jesus walked into the river. "I want you to baptize me too," he said to John. John was shocked. Jesus had never done anything wrong! "No! You should baptize me!" John told Jesus.

"It is right for you to do this," Jesus replied.

John dipped Jesus in the water.

At that moment, the skies opened up, and God's spirit came down from heaven like a dove. A voice said, "This is my Son. I love him, and I am very happy with him!"

God's power shows through Jesus.
God's power works in your life too.

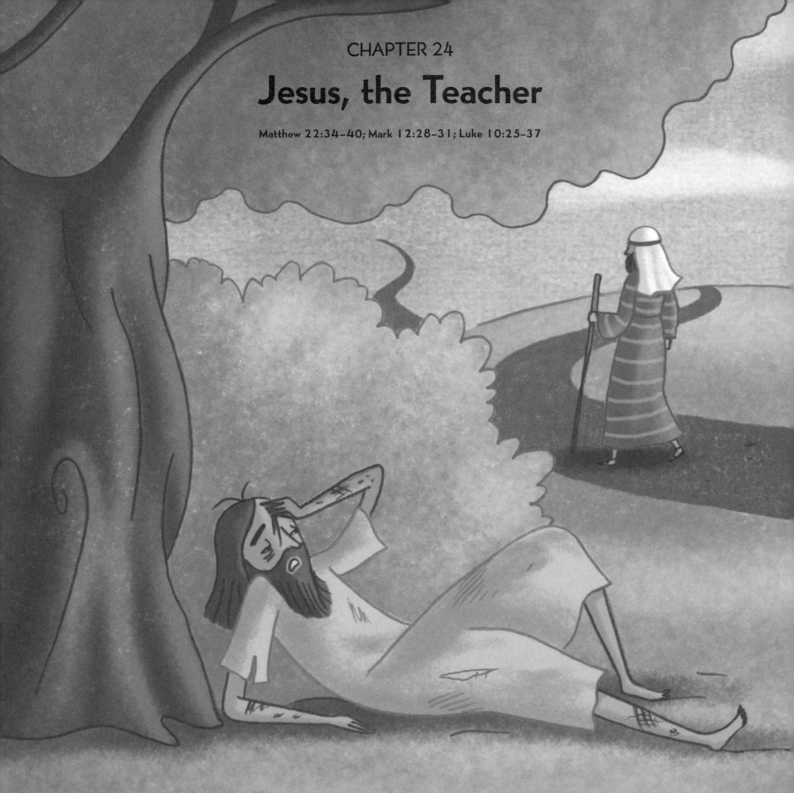

CHAPTER 24
Jesus, the Teacher

Matthew 22:34–40; Mark 12:28–31; Luke 10:25–37

Jesus told the people, "Love God, and love your neighbor as much as you love yourself."

A man asked Jesus, "Who is my neighbor?" Jesus answered his question with this story.

"One day, a man was walking down the road. Suddenly, some robbers jumped out. They hit the man, stole everything he had, and ran away, leaving him lying in the dirt. Soon, a priest came along, but he passed by without helping. Then a leader in the church came along. He didn't stop to help either.

"Finally, a Samaritan came down the road. When he saw the injured man, he felt sorry for him and quickly jumped off his donkey and ran over to help. The Samaritan bandaged the man's sores, put him on his donkey, and took him to an inn where he could get better."

Then Jesus asked, "Who was a neighbor to the injured man?"

The man replied, "The Samaritan who helped him."

Jesus said, "Yes. Be kind, like that man."

Jesus told stories to teach people.
You can learn from Jesus' stories too.

CHAPTER 25

Jesus and the Little Children

Matthew 19:13–15; Mark 10:13–16; Luke 18:15–17

Jesus had helpers called disciples. Jesus taught his disciples everything he knew about God's love.

One day, some families were walking along when they saw Jesus and his disciples resting on a hillside.

"It's Jesus!" the children shouted happily. The boys and girls eagerly ran to Jesus, but the disciples blocked their way.

"You must leave Jesus alone," one of the disciples said.

"Yes, he needs to rest," another added.

"Let the children come to me!" Jesus called to his disciples. "Please don't turn them away!" And with a smile as warm as sunshine, he opened his arms wide and the children went running to him, laughing.

Jesus turned to his disciples. "Do you see these children? If you want to enter God's kingdom, this is how you should come to him—as happy and as trusting as a little child."

Jesus loved the little children.
Jesus loves you too!

CHAPTER 26

Jesus' Sacrifice

Matthew 26–27; Mark 14–15; Luke 22–23; John 13–19

During the festival in Jerusalem, Jesus had a special dinner with his disciples. Jesus took bread and broke it into pieces. He gave the pieces of bread to his disciples. "With this bread, remember me," he said. Jesus gave a cup of wine to his friends. "With this cup, remember me."

Then Jesus went to a garden to pray. He knew something bad was going to happen because he had told people about God's kingdom.

The rulers were worried that Jesus was trying to become king. They decided to get rid of Jesus. Soon soldiers came and arrested him.

Jesus was put on a cross. Before he died, he prayed for the people who hurt him. Jesus said, "Forgive them, Father. They do not understand about God's kingdom."

Jesus died for our sins so we can live
with him in heaven someday.

CHAPTER 27
Jesus Has Risen!

Matthew 28; Mark 16; Luke 24; John 20–21

Jesus was buried in a cave. A huge rock covered the opening. Two days after Jesus died, Mary Magdalene and her friends came to the cave. The earth began to shake. An angel came down from heaven and rolled back the rock.

"Jesus is not here. He has risen!" the shining angel said.

Mary and the others looked inside. Jesus was gone! They ran off to tell Jesus' disciples the wonderful news. "Jesus is alive!" Mary told the men. Everyone was so happy!

Jesus' disciples gathered together in a house. Suddenly, Jesus was there with them! "Peace be with you," Jesus said.

Jesus' disciples couldn't believe their eyes. Some of them did not think Jesus was real.

"Give me some fish," Jesus said.

Jesus ate the fish to show them that he really was alive. His disciples were filled with joy!

God gave Jesus new life.
He can give you a new life too, if you ask him.

CHAPTER 28
The Holy Spirit

Acts 2

Many people were in Jerusalem. They were visiting from other countries. Jesus' disciples were there too.

Suddenly, a powerful wind whooshed and whirled through the room where the disciples were praying. The men looked at each other with wonder. A little flame of fire rested on each of their heads!

128

The disciples were filled with God's spirit of love and peace. When they opened their mouths to speak, their words came out in different languages. They could speak in languages they had never even learned! It was the Holy Spirit who helped them do this.

A crowd of people heard the noise and rushed over to see what was happening. Each one heard their own language being spoken.

The disciples told everyone about Jesus.

"Jesus came to help all people. Follow him and you will be filled with God's spirit!"

Three thousand people were baptized that day!

God gives his followers the Holy Spirit.
The Holy Spirit can live inside you too.

CHAPTER 29

God Uses Paul

Acts 16:16–40

Saul did not like people who followed Jesus. He wanted to put them in jail. On his way to arrest some of the followers, a big, bright light flashed in the sky. Saul fell to the ground. He was blind! A voice said, "Saul! Saul! Why are you against me?" It was Jesus talking to him.

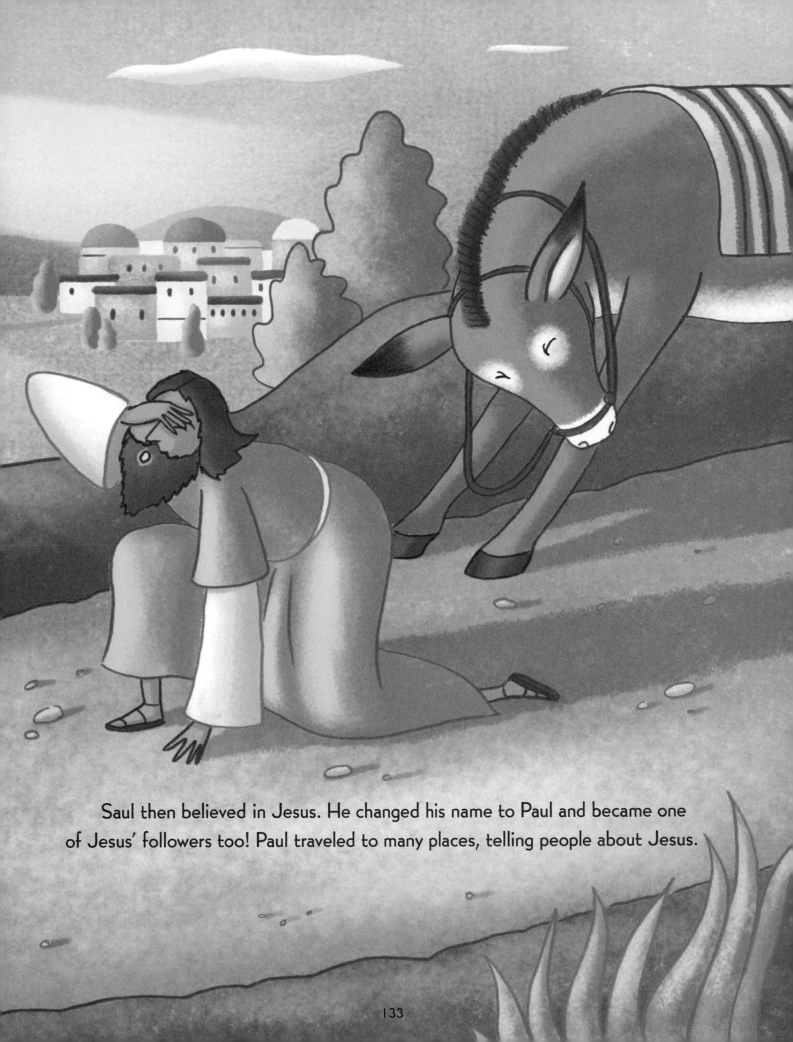

Saul then believed in Jesus. He changed his name to Paul and became one of Jesus' followers too! Paul traveled to many places, telling people about Jesus.

One day, Paul and his helper Silas were put in prison. But Paul and Silas were not afraid. They sang songs to God and prayed.

Suddenly, the ground shook so hard the prison doors flew open. The jailer rushed in, shaking with fear. He let Paul and Silas out of jail and asked them, "What do I have to do to be saved?"

Paul told the jailer, "Believe in the Lord Jesus!"

The jailer took Paul and Silas to his house. He and his family believed in Jesus and were baptized.

Jesus helped Paul and Silas
because they believed in him.
You can believe in Jesus too.

CHAPTER 30

God's Servant

Acts 27

Paul traveled for many years, teaching people about Jesus.

One day, Paul was on a ship when the wind began to blow. Paul told the ship's captain they should stop because a bad storm was coming. The captain did not listen to Paul and kept sailing out to sea.

Soon rain poured down and waves tossed the boat! It was so dark no one could see the sun or the stars. The people on the boat were very scared.

Paul talked to God. Then he told everyone that the ship would be destroyed, but all the people would be safe.

Paul was right. The boat crashed near an island. The people reached the shore safely. Everyone thanked God for saving them.

Paul told everyone he met about Jesus. He wrote many letters to friends. Because of Paul, many people learned about Jesus.

Everything Paul did, he did for God.
You can do things for God too!

CHAPTER 31

Jesus' Return

Revelation 21–22

A man named John was a good friend of Jesus. He became a leader of the church. John told many people about Jesus. This made some of the rulers mad. They took John to an island and made him live there all alone.

John was not afraid. "God is with me!" he said.

God showed John what heaven was like. There were castles and streets of gold. Everyone in heaven was happy. They all sang and worshipped God.

John wrote about the things he saw. He told everyone that one day Jesus would come back to take his children to heaven to live with him forever.

**Because you are a child of Jesus,
you will be with Jesus forever in heaven!**

Trading Cards for Preschoolers

This set of thirty-one trading cards corresponds with The Story for Little Ones and The Story curriculum and is sure to be a hit with preschoolers. Each card depicts a scene or character from the Bible with a Bible verse and important facts on the back. Designed to help with Scripture memorization.

22

"I bring you good news of great joy ... a Savior has been born to you. He is Christ the Lord."

Luke 2:10-11, NIrV

Jesus Is Born

Jesus was born in a stable. Mary and Joseph wrapped him in cloth to keep him warm. God put a star in the sky, and shepherds cam...

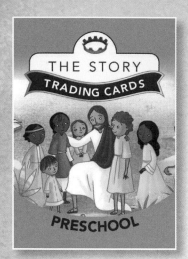

THE STORY TRADING CARDS

PRESCHOOL

JOSEPH

RUTH

BABY JESUS

For Children 4 and up

The Story for Children
A Storybook Bible

This isn't just another collection of Bible stories—it's The Story—the big picture of God's enormous love for his children! Presented by bestselling author and pastor Max Lucado, Randy Frazee, and Karen Hill, these forty-eight pivotal stories show how God has a great and grand and glorious vision, beginning with Creation and ending with the promise that Jesus is coming again. Each story is personalized with God's Message and accompanied by vibrant illustrations that help bring the Bible to life for readers young and old.

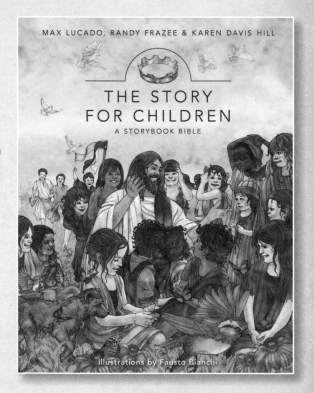

MAX LUCADO, RANDY FRAZEE & KAREN DAVIS HILL

THE STORY FOR CHILDREN
A STORYBOOK BIBLE

Illustrations by Fausto Bianchi

Trading Cards

There are also trading cards for the elementary level that are perfect for reinforcing the Bible stories shared in The Story for Children. Children will enjoy having all thirty-one cards to help them memorize Scripture and learn important facts about the Bible.

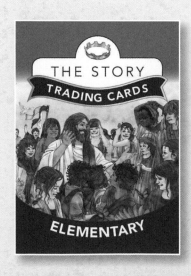

THE STORY TRADING CARDS

ELEMENTARY

THE STORY

Church families around the globe can now embrace The Story for a full ministry year through worship services, small group studies, and family activities. Learn more about this whole-church experience at TheStory.com.

Use this QR Code with your mobile device. Or access directly at **http://zph.com/qr61/**